Best in the World

Illustrated by Martin Remphry

You do not need to read this page - just get on with the book!

First published in 2004 in Great Britain by
Barrington Stoke Ltd, Sandeman House, Trunk's Close,
55 High Street, Edinburgh EH1 1SR

Copyright © 2004 Chris Powling
Illustrations © Martin Remphry

The moral right of the author has been asserted in
accordance with the Copyright, Designs and
Patents Act 1988

ISBN 1-842992-05-8

Printed in Great Britain by Bell & Bain Ltd

MEET THE AUTHOR – CHRIS POWLING

What is your favourite animal?
Cats. I have two at home (Jack and Max)
What is your favourite boy's name?
Jake – the name of my new grandson
What is your favourite girl's name?
Scarlett – the name of a future granddaughter
(I hope!)
What is your favourite food?
Haddock and mashed potatoes
What is your favourite music?
Solo piano (all kinds ... classical
to jazz)
What is your favourite hobby?
I've been a supporter of Charlton
Athletic FC for almost half a century

MEET THE ILLUSTRATOR – MARTIN REMPHRY

What is your favourite animal?
Loch Ness Monster
What is your favourite boy's name?
Edwig
What is your favourite girl's name?
Drucilla
What is your favourite food?
Curry
What is your favourite music?
Mouth organ
What is your favourite hobby?
Playing the harmonica

For Jake ...
when he's old enough

Contents

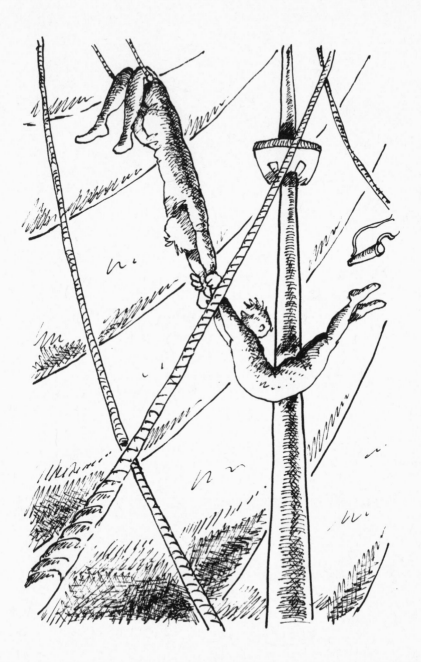

Chapter 1
Now or Never

Jeb had never been so scared.

Even his brother Lucas had gone quiet. There he stood on the platform opposite. And now he was swinging his trapeze towards Jeb's platform. Jeb watched it as it swung to and fro.

Down-and-up.

Down-and-up.

Down-and-up.

Somehow, the gap between them looked wider than ever. So did the drop down to the circus ring. Jeb licked his lips. He struggled to stop himself getting tense.

"Ready?" Lucas called.

"Nearly ..." Jeb choked.

"Nearly?" frowned Lucas. "What's nearly? Either you're ready or you're not. Which is it?"

"I'm ... I'm trying to get this right."

"Trying?"

Lucas gave a snort of disgust. It sounded as loud as a pistol shot in the huge, empty tent. "Forget trying, Bruv," he told Jeb. "Trying is for losers. Just *do* it, OK?"

"Just *do* it," Jeb said softly to himself.

But he couldn't do it. Not yet. Not till his hands had stopped trembling. Not till his heart was beating more normally. He looked down at the safety net. Was it really wide and strong enough? What if he missed it when he fell?

Wasn't this what had happened to Dad?

Jeb still dreamt about his father's accident. Night after night, it came back to him. He watched Dad falling, falling. Jeb watched him grab at, and miss, the safety net. Then came the crunch as he hit the ground. After that, there was a long silence.

Dad lay crooked and broken in the circus ring. Slowly, the sawdust soaked up his blood. At this point, Jeb always woke up screaming.

He wanted to scream right now.

But Lucas was watching him closely. So was Della, their little sister. Jeb could see her peeping through the curtains at the back of the ring. She knew exactly what they were doing. She'd never believe he could back off now.

Jeb took a deep breath. "OK, Bruv," he said. "It's now or never, I reckon."

"Great," said Lucas. "For a moment there, I thought you'd lost it. Still going for the Big One, are we?"

"The Big One," Jeb nodded.

Lucas grinned. "The Big One it is, then," he said. "After that you'll be a real flyer, Jeb. And I'll be a real catcher. Who knows, we may even get an offer from *Circusland*."

"From *Circusland*?"

"Why not, Bruv? With any luck, their talent scout will come and watch us. He'll have seen our act and he'll want it in their show. The Big One makes you the best in the world!"

The best in the world ...

Yes, that's what the Big One made you. Everyone who ever worked in a circus would agree with that. The Big One had made their father the best in the world, Jeb remembered.

Until, in the end, it had killed him.

Chapter 2
The Big One

The Big One ...

In those days, that's what everyone called that daring leap from trapeze to trapeze. Its other name was the Triple. The Triple was three complete spins in mid-air at the highest point of the circus tent.

Think of a head over heels done backwards at lightning speed.

Now multiply it by three.

That's the Triple.

No wonder Jeb was in a sweat. His timing had to be perfect when he let go of his trapeze. So did the angle of his body. Any mistake and Lucas wouldn't be able to catch him. Jeb would fall like a stone towards the safety net. Unless he missed it altogether like Dad had done.

Jeb pushed that thought out of his mind. "Just *do* it, OK?" he whispered.

"Nice and easy, Bruv," said Lucas softly.

By now, each of them was swinging full stretch on his trapeze. Jeb hung the right way up – his feet pointing down to the ring. Lucas hung upside down by his knees from *his* trapeze. They needed to time it just right. A split second more, or a split second less, might be fatal. Their shadows skittered across the great dome of the tent.

"Nice and easy ..." muttered Lucas.

"Just do it!" Jeb was hissing to himself.

Then he let go.

FLIP-FLIP-FLIP! went the Triple.

SMACK! went their hands as they locked together.

SWISH! went the wires of Lucas's trapeze as it carried them both to safety.

Jeb landed on his brother's platform with a neat twist in the air. Lucas joined him a moment later. They stared at each other, wide-eyed. It was hard to believe what had happened. "Was that the Big One, Bruv? The Triple?" Jeb asked. "Did we really do the Triple?"

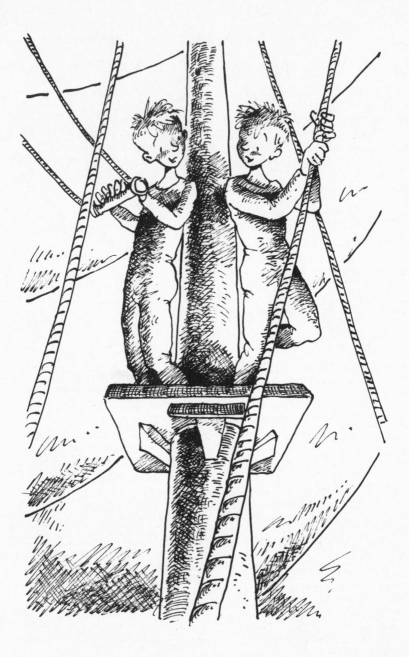

"You bet we did!" grinned Lucas.

"Does that mean ..."

Lucas laughed and shook his head. "It means we're on the right track, that's all."

"But we've just done the Triple!"

"Once," said Lucas. "We've done it *once*, Jeb. Now comes the real work. We've got to practise, practise, practise till we can do it whenever we like. We must make it as natural as breathing. After that, we can include it in our act."

"And then what, Bruv?" asked Jeb.

"Then we wait for the news to spread."

"Will it spread as far as *Circusland?*"

"Who knows?" Lucas winked.

"I know!" someone shouted up to them. "I know!"

It was Della down in the circus ring. She was already dressed in her clown costume for the evening show. They could see the painted smile on her face as she punched the air with excitement. "You're the best in the world!" she was calling. "Do you hear what I'm saying, twins? That was the most amazing trick I've ever seen! You're the best-best-best in the world!"

Chapter 3
Midnight

At last the circus was quiet.

Not all quiet, of course. There were still a few noises if you listened hard. The grunts of the sleeping animals, for instance. Or the flap of canvas in the wind. You could even hear the throb of an electric generator deep in the dark. But, mostly, it was time to relax. Now the chatting could begin ... and the gossip.

"And what is it we gossip about once we're back in our caravans?" Della laughed. "Why, it's always the same. We talk about life in the circus!"

"It's the only life we know," Mum said.

"But it's a great life, Mum!"

"So it is, Del."

Mum was brushing her red ringmaster's coat as she spoke. She did this every night before bed. The coat must be crisp and spotless for tomorrow's performance. It was Mum who held the whole show together. Della knew, too, that it was Mum who'd held the family together since Dad died.

Della bit her lip. "Er ... Mum?" she began.

"Yes, love?"

"I've been thinking about Jeb and Lucas ..."

"Go on," said Mum. "Spit it out."

"They've been practising a new trick," said Della, quickly.

"The Triple?"

"You know about it?"

"It was always going to happen one day, Del. Their dad couldn't resist the Triple, either. They're just like their dad, that pair."

"So you're not going to stop them?"

"Would you?" Mum asked.

Della thought for a moment.

She remembered how she'd felt when she was watching her brothers. It had all been over so quickly. The Triple had lasted no more than the blink of an eye. But during that blink of an eye, she'd glimpsed the very best ... the best in the world.

Who could possibly stop talent like that?

Mum smiled and put her arm round her daughter. "I learnt to live with the Triple years ago," she said. "It's a case of having to if you've got trapeze artists in the family."

"But isn't it dangerous, Mum?"

"It's the most dangerous trick in the circus."

"Why do people do it, then?"

"Because that's how some people are. They can't help testing themselves to the limit. They drive the fastest racing cars. They climb the highest mountains. They rush into the sort of danger that has most of us running away. The risks are part of what attracts them. It makes them feel more alive."

"Are Jeb and Lucas like that, Mum?"

"So are you, I expect."

"Me?"

"Don't look so surprised, Del. You've been up on the trapeze already, haven't you? When you thought I wasn't looking? Trying to copy your brother's tricks?"

"Why haven't you tried to stop me?"

"Would it have worked?"

"No," Della said.

"Exactly," said Mum. "I'm afraid it runs in the family. You've got trapeze work in your blood. If that's what you fancy doing, one day you must go for it. You'll hate yourself if you don't. You mustn't let Dad's accident put you off. He was unlucky, that's all. Unlucky ... and maybe a bit reckless, too."

"Reckless?"

"Dad was tired out the night he died," Mum said. "It was right at the end of the circus season. He badly needed a rest. I begged him to play safe for once and at least drop the Triple from his act. He refused. He just wouldn't listen."

"Why?"

"Because he felt that would be cheating. Besides, there was someone special in the audience ..."

"Who was that?"

"Someone he'd been waiting for all his life – a talent scout from *Circusland*. Even in those days, *Circusland* was the finest show of them all. Dad knew he was tired out. But he couldn't bear to miss his chance."

"Except he did miss it," Della whispered.

After this, neither of them spoke for a while. Mum went back to brushing her tail coat. Della sat with her chin cupped in her hands, thinking. What would Jeb and Lucas have done in Dad's place, she wondered? Would they have played safe to please Mum? Or been just as stubborn as Dad?

What would she have done herself?

For once, she was glad to be away from the circus ring. The caravan felt warm and safe. But even here she could just make out other noises. One was the grunts of the sleeping animals. Another was the flap of canvas in the wind. Why, she could even hear the swish of a trapeze if she listened hard.

The swish of a trapeze?

At once, Della sat up straight. So that's what Jeb and Lucas were doing. Everyone else in the circus had settled down for the night. But not her brothers. Right now, in the Big Top, the twins were still working on the Triple.

Chapter 4
Last Rehearsal

Soon, everyone in the circus knew the twins were practising the Triple. "The Triple?" some of them said. "You mean the trick that killed their father?"

"That trick, yes."

"But nobody does the Triple nowadays. They'll end up as dead as he is if they're not careful."

"How can you be careful when you're spinning head over heels in mid-air? It's nothing to do with being careful. Jeb and Lucas are really talented, no doubt about that. But so was their dad. And his talent didn't save him."

"At least he was the best in the world."

"For a while, maybe. Till he did the Triple once too often. If you ask me, it's not worth the risk."

"Unless it's *Circusland* you're after."

"Yeah ... except for that."

It was the dream of every circus performer to appear one day at *Circusland*. Footballers dream of Old Trafford. Tennis players dream of Wimbledon. Cricketers dream of The Oval. *Circusland* was just as special. You had to be a top performer before their talent scout would even look at you.

This worried Della a bit. "It's as if the twins are living everyone's dream," she told her best friend Monsieur Bonn. "Does it matter that much?"

Monsieur Bonn smiled. He'd been teaching a new trick to his poodles, Jules and Poupette. Now he looked up as the twins turned yet another somersault in the air. "Just watch them," he said. "It's beautiful, no? You see skill like that and you forget all the hardships."

"That's what Mum says," Della said, with a sigh.

The circus had plenty of hardships, after all. Some nights, the Big Top was only half full. On others, the show was held up by protestors. "Animal rights! Animal rights!" they yelled. What made these people such experts, Della wanted to know? Couldn't they see how well animals were treated in a circus? Animals were part of the circus family.

There were other problems, too. Every so often, a town council would ban the circus altogether. "Who wants that kind of mess?" they sniffed. "A circus is nothing but a danger to health and it looks awful, too." Sometimes they sent in a team to inspect the circus. Everything would stop while the inspectors checked out every single detail from safety to schooling.

"Can you read, little girl?" one inspector had snapped at Della.

In fact, she wasn't much of a reader. This was true of most circus people. A lot of the time, they were far too busy to pick up a book. But that didn't mean they couldn't read. Della fixed the inspector with an icy stare. "Well, my English is better than my French," she told him, "though I do find Russian a bit hard."

That shut him up. He must have forgotten that circus performers come from all over the world. Or maybe he didn't care. Perhaps he was the kind of person who wants all of life to be the same.

Suddenly, she felt Monsieur Bonn grab her arm. "Don't look, my dear!" he hissed.

"But I *am* looking," wailed Della.

She'd seen Jeb's mistake already. Or was it Lucas's fault? At any rate, the twins had somehow crashed in mid-air. Now they were falling, falling. Even Jules and Poupette were frozen in horror.

Was this a repeat of Dad's accident?

No, not quite. The brothers landed upside down in the safety net, one after the other. At once, it bounced them upright again. They were grinning broadly as they clambered down to the circus ring. "See what I mean, Jeb?" said Lucas, dusting off his costume. "We needed a tumble like that to get us over our fear of falling. I really think we're ready now ..."

"Ready for the Triple, Bruv?"

"As ready as we'll ever be. We mustn't risk going stale. Let's include it in our next performance."

"Tonight, you mean?"

"Tonight?" Della whispered.

"Hush," murmured Monsieur Bonn.

He could see the twins were already fixed on the evening show. They left the tent arm in arm with a faraway look in their eyes. They didn't even notice their sister, or the Frenchman, or his poodles yapping with excitement.

Chapter 5
Showtime

That afternoon it started to rain. It was still raining at teatime. By evening, it looked as if it would rain forever. "Will *anyone* be coming to the show tonight?" Della asked.

"Not many," said Mum. "Not in this weather."

"So the twins may not ..."

"Do the Triple?"

Mum stopped polishing her shiny, knee-length boots. "Well, it's not a good night for it, Del. You need to be really up for a trick like that. But if Jeb and Lucas have made up their minds ..."

"They have," Della said.

She pressed her nose against the caravan window. She could see the lights of the Big Top shining fuzzily through the rain. *Why not wait for a better day?* she wondered. *Why waste the Triple on a handful of damp, grumpy customers who were already wishing they'd stayed at home?*

Lucas knew the answer to that. He seemed to fill every corner of the twin's caravan as he glared down at his brother. "We're professionals," he growled. "We do our job properly. We're paid to give our very best performance, however small the audience."

"Including the Triple?" Jeb frowned.

"That's part of our best performance, isn't it? The people who've bothered to come out on a night like this deserve the Triple more than anyone! Isn't that what Dad would be telling us?"

"Yeah, but Dad's—"

"Don't say it!" Lucas snapped.

Jeb could see he was getting nowhere. Besides, didn't he agree with his brother, deep down? "OK," he said. "We'll go ahead as planned, then. I only hope they see how good our act is ... the dozen or so people who bother to turn up."

He was right about the size of the
audience. There were only enough people to
fill the first two rows round the circus ring.
Mostly these were families who lived close
by – plus a class from the local primary
school. Only one person had arrived on his
own. He was sitting next to the gangway
with his raincoat collar turned up. On his
lap were some papers he'd taken from his
smart black case. Plainly, he was there to
kill off an hour or two on a cold, wet
evening.

Soon, even he was hooked.

The circus had never been more magical.
It was as if everyone – the ringmaster, the
clowns, the acrobats and the animals (most
of all Jules and Poupette) – was getting
ready for the Triple. You could sense it in
the air like a distant roll of drums.
"Something wonderful is going to happen,"
whispered a kid in the front row.

"Keep watching!" hissed his dad.

"Keep watching!" ran the message from seat to seat. "Something wonderful is going to happen!"

The twins had never felt such stress. As they came to the end of their act, they knew they had to do the Triple. There was only one way to finish now. Up on his platform, Lucas struggled to think clearly. "Nice and easy ..." he warned.

"Just do it!" Jeb gritted his teeth.

Down-and-up.

Down-and-up.

Down-and-up.

Soon, each twin was in position – a hand-grip suspending one of them, a

knee-grip the other. Their trapezes swung closer and closer in the spotlights ...

Finally, Jeb let go.

FLIP-FLIP-FLIP went the Big One – three complete spins in *mid-air*, done backwards at lightning speed, where the circus tent was at its highest.

SMACK! came the locking of hands.

SWISH! went the wires of Lucas's trapeze as the brothers swung back to safety.

"Three spins?" someone shouted.

"Was that the famous Triple?" gasped someone else. "We've seen the Triple after all these years?"

There wasn't a huge uproar once they'd finished, it's true. It's hard for a handful of people to make that much noise – even if they have seen the best in the world. Still, they did what they could. The families shouted till they lost their voices. The school children whistled so loudly their teacher gave up trying to hush them. As for the man in the raincoat ... he leapt to his feet in excitement. His papers spilled over the gangway like litter scattered in the wind.

Della had never been so proud of her brothers. She'd never been so proud of the circus, either.

How could *Circusland* ignore them now?

Chapter 6
Waiting for *Circusland*

"So, what's the delay?" Della grumbled.

"Five days?" said Monsieur Bonn.

"Also five more Triples – six if we count the extra performance yesterday afternoon. *Circusland* must know about it by now. Haven't they seen the reports in the newspapers? And what about all the times we've been on TV this week?"

"Wait a little longer, my dear."

Della hugged Jules and Poupette even tighter. Sitting there, on the steps of Monsieur Bonn's caravan, she'd been struck by a thought. "Er ... Monsieur Bonn?"

"Yes?"

"Do you think he's been here already?"

"The talent scout?"

"He could have come any time this week, couldn't he?" said Della, sadly. "Maybe he's already decided that *Circusland* doesn't need the Triple."

"My dear, that's not possible."

"Why?"

"Because *Circusland* is the best in the world. And the Triple is the best trick in the world. The two are made for each other. Your brothers have been superb every single night, Della. And so have the rest of us, thanks to them!"

This was true. Somehow, the Triple had cheered them all up. Since that first rainy evening, the whole circus was in high spirits. It was as if Jeb and Lucas had lifted them to a different level. There were more people coming to see them, too, as the news began to spread. Last night, every seat in the Big Top had been sold – with long queues at the box office to buy advance tickets. "The show finishes with the Triple!" people were saying.

"That's dangerous, isn't it?"

"Dangerous? The Triple can be a *killer*. It's like a head over heels done backwards – three times over! Except way off the ground, of course."

"They must have practised it for months."

"For years, more than likely. It takes nerves of steel, they say, as well as split-second timing. Guess what, though. They're only a couple of teenagers!"

"Someone told me their father ..."

"I heard that, too."

Della shivered when she remembered this conversation. She'd been "warming the crowd" at the time. This meant clowning up and down the gangways while the Big Top was filling up with people. The twins, and their Triple, had become the high point of the show all right – in more ways than one.

So why no message from *Circusland*?

She stared glumly across the campsite at her brothers' caravan. That's when she saw Lucas coming towards them. He had a piece of paper in his hand. Monsieur Bonn was already on his feet. He was holding back Jules and Poupette who seemed to sense this was something important.

Della found she couldn't move.

Lucas was trying to smile. His cheeks were flushed, though, and his eyes had an odd brightness. "It's arrived," he said, huskily. "The letter we've all been waiting for."

"From *Circusland*?" his sister whispered.

"They're sending their scout to see us perform. He's coming to the show tonight."

"Lucas, that's wonderful news!"

"No, it isn't," said her brother, bitterly. "It's the worst news we've ever had."

"Why do you say that?"

"Just look at me, Sis. Can't you see the state I'm in? It must've been all that rain at the beginning of the week. I've got a really high temperature. I can hardly breathe. My chest feels like it's on fire and my eyes are streaming ..."

"You mean—"

"Della, I've got 'flu."

Chapter 7
Disaster

"Mum, stop them!" Della begged.

"I can't," said Mum. "They're just the same as their father. If they miss a chance like this they'll never forgive themselves. They'll never forgive me, either."

"But Lucas hasn't even seen a doctor!"

"A doctor would never let him perform in his state, Della. Everyone understands that. And everyone understands why the twins feel they can't back down ..."

"*Circusland*," Della said.

"It's the best in the world," said Mum in a tense voice.

"So that makes it worth the risk?"

"What do you think?"

Della looked away. One of these days it might be her turn to do the Triple. Anyway, she'd seen how upset everyone was when they heard that Lucas was ill. "It's only a cold, after all," they'd mumbled. "A few sniffles can't be fatal, can they?"

Well, perhaps they could.

And if you added a high temperature, a chest that was on fire, a nose that streamed like a tap, and if every breath you took felt like your last …

But nobody wanted to think about that. Lucas least of all. Not in front of the biggest crowd they'd ever had in the Big Top. Not after the best show they'd ever performed – a show everyone agreed was fit to be seen at *Circusland*.

Now only the Triple was left.

It was the climax of the evening. Even the tiny white-faced clown and her mother, the cool, elegant ringmaster could hardly bear the suspense. Along with everyone else, they gave a sigh of relief when the brothers began their warm-up routine.

Was the warm-up taking longer than usual?

Just showmanship, they decided. Just building up the suspense. Only Jeb knew that Lucas had nearly dropped him twice already. At this height, only he could see the sweat on his brother's brow and hear the wheezing rattle in his throat. So far they'd been lucky ... with the easier tricks.

How much longer could they put off the hardest one?

Down-and-up.

Down-and-up.

Down-and-up ...

... went Lucas's trapeze.

Yet still he went on rocking it. He seemed to be moving in a dream, lulled by the swish of the trapeze wires through the cool night air. He made no attempt to leave his platform.

Jeb stared at his brother, puzzled. Surely Lucas knew how hard it was for a flier to keep his nerve with such a delay? Already Jeb felt a tingling down his spine and a tensing of his muscles. Much more of this and he'd be stuck there, unable to move. "Come on!" he heard himself whisper.

"Come on!" urged the crowd below.

Slowly, Lucas shook his head.

He reached for the safety rope. He tucked this neatly between his ankles. He climbed down to the ground as gracefully as any dancer. He walked halfway across the circus ring before people understood the show was over. There was going to be no Triple tonight, no matter how long they'd waited.

At first there was a stunned silence.

Then the catcalls began.

After this came wave after wave of booing.

In the end, someone threw a programme into the ring. Soon, a host of fluttering, spinning programmes flopped onto the sawdust like birds coming home to roost. By now, the jeers and the snarls and the hooting were far louder than the noise any circus animals could make. In the middle of all this uproar only one person sat perfectly still.

It was the talent scout from *Circusland*.

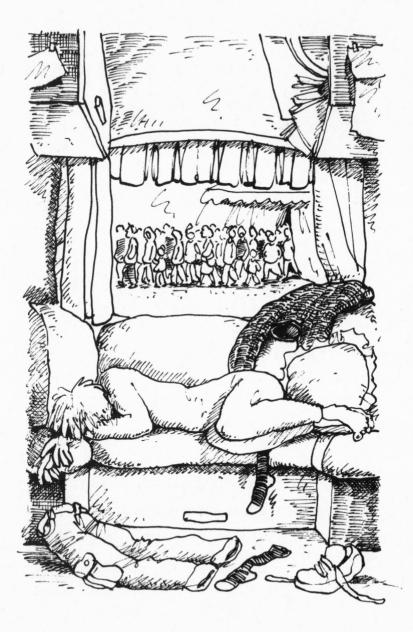

Chapter 8
Best in the World

Lucas slumped on a bench in his caravan. His head hurt. His chest hurt. Just about every muscle in his body hurt. The hurt inside him was the worst, though.

Of course, nobody in the circus would blame him for what he'd done. In fact, they'd be careful to leave him alone till he was ready to face the world again. Even Jeb and Mum and Della would stay away for a while. "We had to get on with our jobs after the show," they'd explain. "We couldn't come to see you. Someone's got to clear up, after all ..."

"Except someone with 'flu," Lucas groaned. "Or someone who's just messed up."

KNOCK! KNOCK!

Lucas forced himself to his feet. Every step he took across the caravan made his head spin. The freshness of the night air outside almost made him gag. "Who's there?" he asked, as he peered into the darkness.

"Can you spare me a moment, young man? It won't take long, I promise. Here's my card."

"Your card?"

Lucas stared at its neat, thin print. He could just about read it in the dim light of the lamp:

```
S. Lee
Talent Scout
CIRCUSLAND
```

"I think you've been expecting me," Mr Lee said.

He ducked his head as he came through the door. Also, he sat in just the right seat. Mr Lee wore a smart suit, and carried a trim black case, but you could see at once he was well used to caravans. "They tell me you're ill," he said. "Is that why you missed the Triple tonight?"

"Something like that."

"Everyone was very upset."

"Look," Lucas sighed. "Nobody was more upset than me, Mr Lee. I'm sorry if I've wasted your time."

"Who says you have? You're not the only act in the circus, young man. Monsieur Bonn and his dogs were wonderful, for example. So was the ringmaster – your mother, I believe. Even your little sister is excellent. I'm hoping all three of them will be appearing at *Circusland* next season."

"Really?" Lucas gasped.

"Yes, really," said Mr Lee. "But I'd still like to know more about you and your brother. It was hard to see what was going on from where I was sitting. Can you tell me what happened?"

Lucas felt embarrassed. He looked away. "Everything felt wrong up there," he said. "My grip, my timing, my reading of Jeb's movements. I was full of 'flu, I suppose. To begin with, I hoped sheer practice would get us through. Then I wasn't so sure. It seemed more and more likely that I'd drop him."

"So you dropped the Triple instead."

"Yes, sir."

"Quite right, too."

"Sir?"

Mr Lee bent forward a little. He tapped a finger on his black case to stress the point he was making. "Young man," he said, "safety must always come first in a circus. We've got enough problems these days without adding accidents to the list."

"Right ..." Lucas said.

"Of course, strictly speaking, you shouldn't have been there at all tonight. Not in your state of health. Maybe my visit had something to do with you going ahead with the act. At least you did the right thing in the end. Also, you were rather brave, I thought. It couldn't have been easy to cancel the Triple at that late stage. Not in front of thousands of people who'd come just to see it."

"I was scared stiff," said Lucas. "And it didn't help much knowing you'd miss our Triple as well, Mr Lee."

"I've already seen it."

"What?"

"I was here earlier this week. On a night so windy and wet the Big Top was nearly empty. You still gave your very best performance, I'm glad to say. So did everyone else in the show. I was so excited by what I saw I got quite carried away. You may remember me spilling my paperwork all over the gangway."

"That was *you?*"

"It certainly was," said the talent scout. "Tonight's visit was simply to check that you and your brother are sensible as well as talented. You certainly showed me that."

"No kidding ..." said Lucas, in a faint voice.

"I've already spoken to Jeb and the others. They tell me they'll all be happy to join us at *Circusland* early in the New Year. Is that your answer, too?"

"You mean it, Mr Lee?"

"Every word, Lucas. You'll be hearing from me next week when the contracts have been drawn up. So will everyone else I've spoken to tonight. And now, I'd advise you to see a doctor. That 'flu of yours needs proper treatment."

Soon after that, with another duck of his head, Mr Lee saw himself out of the caravan. It was just as well he did. Lucas was too stunned to be polite.

As he lay back on the pillow, his head spun more than ever. All round him, out in the pitch-black dark, he could hear the circus sounds he loved so much: the grunts of the sleeping animals, the flap of canvas in the wind – even the throb-throb-throb of an electric generator. Or was this just his heart beating with excitement?

BEST-IN-THE-WORLD

BEST-IN-THE-WORLD

BEST-IN-THE-WORLD

... it seemed to be saying.

Lucas loved that sound most of all.

Barrington Stoke would like to thank all its readers for commenting on the manuscript before publication and in particular:

Robert Clements

Callum Cuthbert

Holly Dunning

Daisy Everett

M. Kleissner

Alexia Kyriaz

John Letsinger

James Norsworthy

Matthew Urch

Become a Consultant!

Would you like to give us feedback on our titles before they are published? Contact us at the address or website below – we'd love to hear from you!

Barrington Stoke, Sandeman House, Trunk's Close, 55 High Street, Edinburgh EH1 1SR
Tel: 0131 557 2020 Fax: 0131 557 6060
E-mail: info@barringtonstoke.co.uk
Website: www.barringtonstoke.co.uk

If you loved this story, why don't you read ...

Grow up, Dad!
by Narinder Dhami
ISBN 1-842992-04-X
£4.99

Do you ever feel like your dad doesn't understand you? Robbie does. His dad just doesn't know how he feels. Until one day, with a bit of magic, things change forever ...

You can order *Grow up, Dad!* directly from our website at www.barringtonstoke.co.uk